W9-CTM-010

English text copyright © 2009 by Jane Kurtz
Illustration copyright © 2009 by Durga Bernhard
Amharic text copyright © 2009 by Bezabeh Belachew

All rights reserved. No part of this publication may be reproduced or transmitted
in any form or by any means, electronic or mechanical, including photocopy,
recording, or any information storage and retrieval system,
without permission in writing from the publisher.

Request for permission to make copies of any part of this work should be mailed to:
Ethiopia Reads, 55 Madison St., Suite 750, Denver, CO 80206

ISBN 978-0-9801483-2-9

Printed in the U.S.A.
Printed by Zemi Design & Print, CO 2009

Stay out of Trouble!
Jane K.

For Daniel and Lily Yohannes
and Abinet Haile,
good roommates and friends
with roots in three countries
—J. K.

For Kalifa Sissoko
—D. B.

Trouble

ተክሴ

Written by Jane Kurtz
Illustrated by Durga Bernhard
Translation by Bezabeh Belachew
ትርጉም በዛብህ በላቸው

Ethiopia Reads
Addis Ababa • Denver

Trouble always found Tekleh. He didn't mean to get stung by poking a stick into a line of marching ants. He didn't mean to make dust fly onto the roasting coffee beans.

ተክሌ ሁሌ ችግር ውስጥ እንደገባ ነው። ያኔ በሰልፍ የሚጓዙትን ጉንዳኖች በእንጨት ሲነካካ ይነክሱኛል ብሎ አላሰበም ነበር። አንዴም ሲጫወት ያቦነው አቢራ የሚቆላው ቡና ውስጥ ይገባል ብሎ ፈጽሞ አልጠበቀም።

And when he watched the family goats, he always meant to tend them carefully.

የቤተሰቡንም ፍየሎች ጠብቅ ሲባል፣ እነሱን በደንብ መንከባከብ ፍላጎቱ ነበር።

Finally, one day, Tekleh's father took a piece of wood and carved a *gebeta* board. "Now," he said, "we will have no more problems. A *gebeta* game always keeps a young boy out of trouble."

አንድ ቀን የተክሌ አባት እንጨት ጠርቦ የገበጣ መጫወቻ ሰራ። አባቱም ‹ስእንግዲህ
ወዲህ ችግሮች አያጋጥሙንም። የገበጣ ጨዋታ ልጆች ችግር ውስጥ እንዳይገቡ
ይጠብቃል፡፡› ብሎ ተናገረ።

The next morning, Tekleh meant to head straight to the goats' grazing place in the hills. But, far in the distance, something was happening on the path.

በማግሥቱ ጠዋት ተክሌ ፍየሎቹን ወደሚያሰማራበት የግጦሽ ኮረብታ ለመሄድ አስቦ ነበር፡ ፡
ነገር ግን መንገዱን ሲጀምር ከሩቁ አንድ ነገር አየ፡ ፡

Ah-hah. It was a group of traders with their dusty, musky camels. "Is there no wood in this country?" one of them asked. "We found only a few sticks for our fire."

"Of course there is wood," Tekleh said. He held up his *gebeta* board.

"Thank you," the man said. He grabbed the board and threw it on the fire.

ለካስ ከአቢራማ ግመሎቻቸው ጋር የሚንዙ ነጋዴዎች ነበሩ፡፡ ከነጋዴዎቹም አንዱ ‹እዚህ አገር እንጨት የለም እንዴ? ለእሳት ማንደጃ ያገኘነው ጭራሮ ብቻ ነው፡፡› ብሎ ተናገረ፡፡

‹እንጨትማ በደንብ አለ በማለት ተክሌ የገበጣ መጫወቻውን ከፍ አድርጎ አሳየው፡፡ ነጋዴውም ‹አመሰግናለው› ብሎ የተክሌን ገበጣ መጫወቻ እሳት ውስጥ ወረወረው፡፡

Tekleh set up such a howling that the traders' ears hurt. "Take this fine knife," one cried, "and stop that noise."

Tekleh was sad, but what could be done now? Down the path he went with his two goats and the fine knife.

ተክሌ የገበጣ መጫወቻው ሲቃጠል ነጋዴዎቹ ጆሮቻውን እስከሚያማቸው ድረስ በሃዘን ጨኸኩቱን ለቀቀ። አንዱም ነጋዴ ጮክ ብሎ ‹ጨኸትክን አቁምና ይህንን ጥሩ ቢላ ውሰድ› አለው።

Before long, he saw a man sitting in the long grass. "Here," the man said. "A knife is not a thing for a young boy. Why don't you let me have it to skin the little *dik-dik* that will soon be caught in my trap?"

ተክሌ በጣም አዝኖ ነበር፡፡ ግን አሁን ምን ማድረግ ይቻላል? ሁለቱ ፍየሎቹንና አዲሱ ቢላውን ይዞ መንገዱን ቀጠለ፡፡

ተክሌ ብዙም ሳይቆይ አንድ ሰው ረጅም ሳር አጠገብ ተቀምጦ አየ፡፡ ሰውየውም ‹ስማ ለትንሽ ልጅ ቢላ ጥሩ አይደለም፡፡ ለምን በወጥመድ የምይዛትን የሚዳቋ ቆዳ እንድገፍበት ለኔ አትሰጠኝም› ብሎ ጠየቀው፡፡

Tekleh was sorry to think of such a shy and delicate animal becoming a meal. But people must eat. So he said, "What will you give me if I give you this fine knife?"

The man held out his *masinko*. "My family needs food more even than music."

ሚዳቋን የመሰለች ትንሽና ሰላማዊ እንስሳ ለሰው ምግብ እንደምትሆን ሲያስብ ተክሌ በጣም አዘነ። ነገር ግን ሰዎች መብላት አለባቸው። ስለዚህም ተክሌ ሰውየውን ‹ይህን ጥሩ ቢላ ብሰጥህ አንተስ ምን ትሰጠኛለህ?› አለው።

ሰውየውም ማሲንቆውን አውጣና ‹ከሙዚቃ የበለጠ ቤተሰቤ የሚያስፈልገው ምግብ ነው› አለ።

So off Tekleh went with his two goats and his *masinko*, making a fine noise, until he came upon a group of musicians shaking their shoulders as they danced. "Why don't you give us that *masinko* to play at the wedding feast?" one said. "You take this drum instead."

ተክሌም ሁለቱን ፍየሎችና ማሲንቆውን ይዞ ጉዞውን ቀጠለ፡፡ በማሲንቆውም ግሩም ዜማ እየተጫወተ ሲጓዝ እስክስታ የሚወርዱ ሰዎች መንገድ ላይ አገኘ፡፡ ከነሱም አንዱ ‹እስቲ ማሲንቆህን ስጠንና የሰርግ ድግስ ላይ እንጫወትበት፡፡ እንካ አንተ ይህን ከበሮ ውሰድ› አለው፡፡

Why not? Tekleh tucked the drum under his arm and tagged after them to the wedding, where the red smell of spices filled the air.

ተክሌ ከበሮውን በጁ አቅፎ ሰዎቹን እየተከተለ ወደ ሠርጉ ሄደ፡፡ አየሩም በቅመማ ቅመም ሽታ ታውዶ ነበር፡፡

In the swirl of music and dancing, no one noticed Tekleh sampling the wedding feast. When one of the cooks finally chased him away, Tekleh trotted off with his two goats and his drum.

ዘፈኑና ጭፈራው ደርቶ ስለነበር ተክሌ የድግሱን ምግብ ሲቀማምስ ማንም አላየውም፡፡ በመጨረሻም ከምግብ አዘጋጆቹ አንዱ ስታባርረው ፍየሎቹንና ከበሮውን ይዞ መሮጥ ጀመረ፡፡

The path was hot, and Tekleh stopped to watch a lizard sunning itself on a rock. His mother had told him not to touch lizards, but this one was so mysterious and still—and it could eat flies and mosquitoes in the house.
So he popped it into his bag.

ተክሌ በሚምቀው መንገድ ሲጓዝ እንድ እንሽላሊት ፀሐይ ሲሞቅ ለማየት ቆመ፡፡ እናቱ
ከዚህ በፊት እንሽላሊት እንዳይነካ አስጠንቅቃው ነበር፡፡ ነገር ግን ይህ እንሽላሊት ልዩ
ይመስላል፤ ቤትም ውስጥ ዝንብና ትንኝ ሊበላ ይችላል ብሎ አሰበ፡፡ ስለዚህ ተክሌ
እንሽላሊቱን ቦርሳው ውስጥ ከተተው፡፡

When he found a shady cornfield, Tekleh took out his drum and began to thump. Three monkeys leaped out of the corn and scampered off. The farmer ran over. "Stay here and make that wonderful noise all afternoon," he said, "and I will give you a bag full of corn."

ቀጥሎም ተክሌ የበቆሎ ማሳ ጥላ ውስጥ ገብቶ ከበሮውን ይመታ ጀመር። የከበሮውን ድምጽ ሲሰሙ ሶስት ጦጣዎች ከበቆሎው እርሻ ወጥተው ይሮጡ ጀመር። ባለ እርሻው ወደ ተክሌ እየሮጠ ሄዶ ‹በል እዚህ ቁጭ በልና ያንን አስደሳች የከበሮ ድምጽ ቀኑን ሙሉ ተጫወት። እኔም አንድ ስልቻ በቆሎ እሰጥሃለው።› አለው።

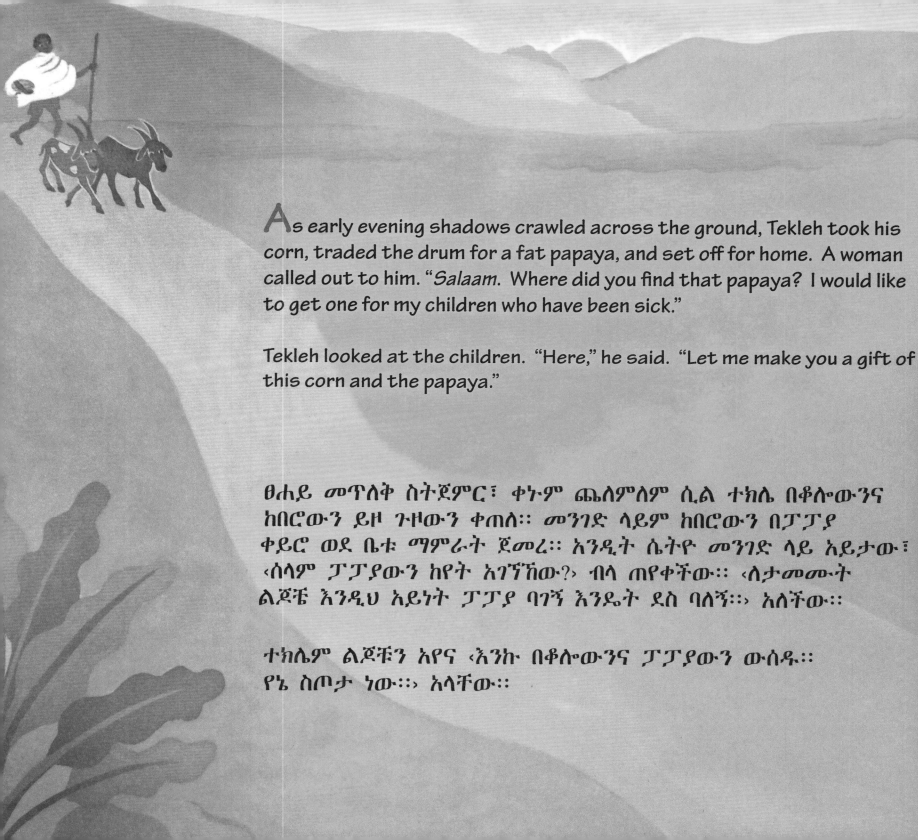

As early evening shadows crawled across the ground, Tekleh took his corn, traded the drum for a fat papaya, and set off for home. A woman called out to him. "*Salaam*. Where did you find that papaya? I would like to get one for my children who have been sick."

Tekleh looked at the children. "Here," he said. "Let me make you a gift of this corn and the papaya."

ፀሐይ መጥለቅ ስትጀምር፤ ቀኑም ጨለምለም ሲል ተክሌ በቆሎውንና ከበሮውን ይዞ ጉዞውን ቀጠለ። መንገድ ላይም ከበሮውን በፓፓያ ቀይሮ ወደ ቤቱ ማምራት ጀመረ። አንዲት ሴትዮ መንገድ ላይ አይታው፤ ‹ሰላም ፓፓያውን ከየት አገኘኸው?› ብላ ጠየቀችው። ‹ለታመሙት ልጆቼ እንዲህ አይነት ፓፓያ ባገኝ እንዴት ደስ ባለኝ።› አለችው።

ተክሌም ልጆቹን አየና ‹እንኩ በቆሎውንና ፓፓያውን ውሰዱ። የኔ ስጦታ ነው።› አላቸው።

"Come in," the woman said. She blew on the fire and stirred the lentils. While Tekleh scooped up the lentils with his *injera*, he watched the children playing their *gebeta* game. Then he coaxed the goats out of the neighbor's garden, said goodbye, and started down the path.

Suddenly, he heard footsteps. The littlest girl was running after him, holding out the *gebeta* board.

ሴትዮዋም ‹ና ወደ ቤት ግባ› ብላ ጠራችው፡፡ እሳቱን ኡፍ ብላ ምስር ወጥ ማማሰል ጀመረች፡፡ ተክሌም ምስሩን በእንጀራ እየበላ ልጆቹ ገበጣ ሲጫወቱ ይመለከት ጀመር፡፡ በልቶም ሲጨርስ ፍየሎቹን ከጎሮ ሰብስቦ ሰዋቹን ተሰናብቶ *መንገዱን* ቀጠለ፡፡

ድንገት ከጀርባው የሰው እርምጃ ሰማ፡፡ ትንሿ ልጅ የገባጣ *መጫወቻቸውን* ልትሰጠው እየተከተለችው ነበር፡፡

So it was that Tekleh came home with two goats, one lizard, and a *gebeta* board. His father patted him on the head with pride.

"How well fed and contented the goats are today," he said to his family. "Did I not tell you? A *gebeta* board never fails to keep a young boy out of trouble."

ተክሌ ሁለት ፍየሎች፣ አንድ እንሽላሊትና፣ አንድ የገበጣ መጫወቻ ይዞ ቤቱ ገባ፡፡ አባቱም በልጁ በጣም ኮርቶ ጭንቅላቱን ይደባብሰው ጀመር፡፡

የተክሌ አባት ‹ዛሬ ፍየሎቹ በደንብ የጠገቡና የተደሰቱ ይመስላሉ› ብሎ ለቤተሰቡ ተናገረ፡፡ ‹ነግሬያችሁ የለ? የገበጣ መጫወቻ ሁሌ ልጅ ችግር ውስጥ እንዳይገባ ይጠብቃል› አላቸው፡፡

GLOSSARY

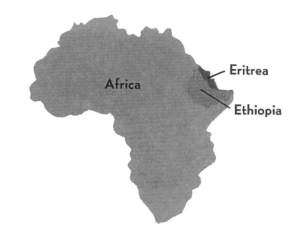

Africa

Eritrea

Ethiopia

dik-dik (dik-dik):
a very small antelope

gebeta (GUH-buh-tuh):
a popular board game played all over the world, also called mancala

injera (in-JE-rah):
a large, spongy pancake used as bread at most meals in Eritrea and Ethiopia

masinko (mah-SINK-oh):
a one-stringed fiddle with a diamond-shaped sound box, a thick horsehair string, and a curved wooden bow

Tekleh (TUK-kuh-luh):
literally translated as "to plant"

Books Change Lives

Ethiopia Reads believes that education is the key to improving the future of Ethiopia. By fostering a genuine love of learning, books bring hope, vision and educational skills to this generation of Ethiopian children.

Ethiopia Reads works to improve literacy and create a culture of reading in Ethiopia. We plant libraries for children, publish books in local Ethiopian languages and train teachers and librarians to nurture a love of reading and books.

A non-profit organization with offices in Denver, Colorado, and Addis Ababa, Ethiopia, Ethiopia Reads is a volunteer-led organization. Sales of this book directly support our literacy programs. Please share this book with friends and family, as well as your local library and school.

Want to get involved or find more ways to help? We'd love to hear from you:
Ethiopia Reads
55 Madison Street, Suite 750
Denver, Colorado 80206
303-468-8422
info@ethiopiareads.org
www.ethiopiareads.org